Magic Pony

♥ Brightheart ♥

WITHDRAWN FROM STOCK

With a jolt, Brightheart's hoofs thudded against the ground. Amy grabbed hold of the front of the saddle. The bump shook away the last of the silvery sparkles that had been whirling around her head. She straightened up, puzzled.

Was this part of the carousel ride?

Then she gasped out loud.

She was riding a real live pony!

Brightheart's coat was no longer painted on. Shaking, Amy put out her hand and touched Brightheart's neck. It felt warm and soft!

But where were they?

Also available
Sparkle

And coming soon
Star
Jewel

Brightheart

Poppy Shire

Illustrated by Strawberrie Donnelly

MACMILLAN CHILDREN'S BOOKS

A Working Partners Book

With special thanks to Holly Skeet

First published 2006 by Macmillan Children's Books
a division of Macmillan Publishers Limited
20 New Wharf Road, London N1 9RR
Basingstoke and Oxford
www.panmacmillan.com

Associated companies throughout the world

ISBN-13: 978-0-330-44042-4
ISBN-10: 0-330-44042-X

Text copyright © Working Partners Limited 2006
Illustrations copyright © Strawberrie Donnelly 2006

Created by Working Partners Limited

The right of Strawberrie Donnelly to be identified as the
illustrator of this work has been asserted by her in
accordance with the Copyright, Designs and Patents Act 1988.

All rights reserved. No part of this publication may be
reproduced, stored in or introduced into a retrieval system, or
transmitted, in any form or by any means (electronic, mechanical,
photocopying, recording or otherwise), without the prior written
permission of the publisher. Any person who does any unauthorized
act in relation to this publication may be liable to criminal
prosecution and civil claims for damages.

1 3 5 7 9 8 6 4 2

A CIP catalogue record for this book is available from
the British Library.

Printed and bound in Great Britain by Mackays of Chatham plc, Kent

Leabharlann
Contae na Midhe

This book is sold subject to the condition that it shall not,
by way of trade or otherwise, be lent, resold, hired out,
or otherwise circulated without the publisher's prior consent
in any form of binding or cover other than that in which
it is published and without a similar condition including this
condition being imposed on the subsequent purchaser.

Contents

1. Fun at the Fairground

"Hurry up, hurry up!" Amy tugged at her grandad's sleeve. She could hear lively music floating down the road from the fairground. She had been saving up her pocket money for weeks and wanted to go on every single ride!

"All right, love, we're nearly there," her grandad protested, his eyes twinkling.

Amy ran towards the park gates. The music was much louder here and butterflies of excitement danced in her tummy. Which ride should she go on first? She tried to join the queue for a rollercoaster that swooped and soared high above the fairground.

But the man taking the money looked at her and shook his head. "Sorry, you're not tall enough. Come back next year!"

Amy felt very disappointed.

Grandad smiled at her and took her hand. "Come on, we can find something else."

They stopped beside a stall where you had to throw plastic hoops over different prizes. Amy was pretty sure she could get a hoop over one of the teddies, but she already had loads of teddies at home.

She shook her head. "The teddies are really cute, but there might be something even better!" she explained to Grandad, and he nodded.

"What about that game over there?" Grandad said. "You'd be great at that!" He pointed to a stall called "Beat the Goalie".

Amy ran over to look. You had to kick a football past a huge inflatable goalkeeper and into different holes to score points. Amy loved playing football. Yesterday she'd scored the winning goal in a match against her team's hottest rivals.

"I'll definitely have a go later," she said. "But I want to try one of the rides first. Something *really* special." She smiled up at her grandad. "I just haven't found it yet!"

Grandad grinned back, and they headed off to find the perfect first fairground ride.

Suddenly, there it was.

In a corner of the field, tucked behind a pink and white striped candyfloss stall, stood an old-fashioned pony carousel. It was painted a rich red, with touches of gold and silver, and a scarlet flag fluttered from the pointy golden roof. Gorgeous wooden ponies cantered round and round, rising and

falling in time to the music on twisty golden poles. As soon as Amy saw it, she knew that *this* was the perfect first ride.

"Grandad, look at those beautiful ponies!" Amy loved riding even more than playing football. Her favourite pony at the local riding stables was a friendly little chestnut mare called Buttons. The carousel ponies looked even lovelier than Buttons, kicking up their heels as though they were desperate to be off. They had flowing manes and tails, and their names were picked out in twinkling gold paint on their harnesses.

Amy ran over to look more closely at the different ponies. There were so many! She could see a dappled grey circus pony called Sparkle, who had feathers nodding on his bridle and a mischievous glint in his eye. Next to Sparkle was a chestnut pony called

Star, with a lasso hanging from his saddle –
he must be a cowgirl's pony!

But there, just behind Star, was the pony
Amy wanted to ride most of all. He was a
magnificent pony with a proudly arched
neck and flaring nostrils. He looked noble
and adventurous, and his big brown eyes
seemed to look straight at Amy, inviting her
to climb aboard. His name-scroll said
Brightheart, and it was the perfect name
for him. Amy's favourite book was
all about knights and princesses, and
Brightheart could have galloped straight
out of its pages. "Hello there! I see you are
admiring my beautiful ponies!"

Amy jumped. A tall gentleman was
smiling down at her. He looked more like a
magician than someone who ran a
fairground ride! He wore a red velvet suit

with a bright green lining, and on his head was a magnificent red and green striped top hat. He bowed to her, sweeping the stripy hat from his head. His jacket flapped open to reveal a flash of brilliant green like a parrot's wing.

"Welcome to Barker's Magic Pony Carousel!" he said.

Amy gasped. "*Magic* Pony Carousel? Are you sure?"

The showman beamed at her. He had thick white hair that stood up in tufts, but his eyes were young and shone with happiness. "Oh yes, I'm sure. After all, *I* am Mr Barker and this is *my* Magic Carousel. Would you like a ticket?"

"I'd *love* one!" Amy bounced up and down on the balls of her feet, feeling as though she was bubbling over with excitement.

Mr Barker pulled a stern face, shaking a finger at her – but his eyes were still twinkling! "I have one very important rule on my carousel. You have to ride the pony whose name is on your ticket."

Amy nodded breathlessly. Which pony's name would be on her ticket? She hoped it would be Brightheart!

Mr Barker reached into the pocket of his red velvet coat. "Hmm, what do we have here? Ah yes!"

With a flourish, he pulled out a huge bunch of flowers!

Amy giggled.

"Goodness me!" Mr Barker looked

8

surprised. "Wherever did those come from? Would you be so kind as to hold them for a moment, sir?"

He handed the flowers to Amy's grandad, who took them with a smile.

"Thank you so much. Now, where did I put that ticket? Aha!" Mr Barker leaned forward and plucked a little pink ticket from behind Amy's ear. She stared at it in astonishment.

"So that's where you were hiding it, is it?" said Mr Barker, smiling. He handed her the ticket.

Amy looked down at it, hardly daring to read the name. But there it was, in beautiful swirly writing.

Brightheart!

Mr Barker's
Magic Pony Carousel

Brightheart

One Ride

2. Medieval Magic

"It says Brightheart!" Amy cried happily.

Mr Barker raised his eyebrows. "Well, isn't that a stroke of luck! On you get, we're ready to start!"

Grandad beamed. "Have a lovely time!" he called.

Amy ran up the steps to the wooden platform where the ponies hovered on their golden poles, their hoofs not quite touching the floor. She weaved through the other ponies until she came to Brightheart.

"Hello, Brightheart," she whispered,

running her hand down his dark neck. The wood felt cold and shiny under her fingers. "I'm really glad it was your name on my ticket!"

The pony's painted brown eyes stared back at her without blinking. Amy put one foot in the gold-painted stirrup and climbed into the side saddle. She had to do a bit of wriggling to get in the right place – but once she was on, it was surprisingly comfy!

Mr Barker was standing in the middle of the carousel. "Is everyone ready? Hold on tight then!" He looked around to make sure everyone was on their ponies. Then, using both hands, he turned a big handle to start the carousel. There was a creaking, grinding noise and the carousel began to spin – slowly at first, then faster and faster.

A merry tune began to play, making Amy want to sing along.

Amy waved to her grandad as she flew past, gripping the pole tightly with her other hand. The colours of the fairground whirled around her and she blinked, trying not to feel dizzy. Brightheart swooped up and down and Amy laughed out loud with excitement.

Suddenly the fairground disappeared in a sea of silvery sparkles. Amy felt as if she was galloping through a glittery mist. The carousel had vanished, and beneath the music she could hear voices and bridles jingling.

What was happening?

With a jolt, Brightheart's hoofs thudded against the ground. Amy grabbed hold of the front of the saddle. The bump shook away the last of the silvery sparkles that had been whirling around her head. She straightened up, puzzled.

Was this part of the carousel ride?

Then she gasped out loud.

She was riding a real live pony!

Brightheart's dark coat was no longer painted on. He had a jingling green leather bridle and a thick black mane. Shaking, Amy put out her hand and touched Brightheart's neck. It felt warm and soft!

But where were they? Amy turned

around and nearly fell off Brightheart in surprise. A huge castle loomed up behind her. It was built of grey stone, like the one her class had studied for a project about the Middle Ages — except this one wasn't ancient and crumbling and full of holes. It looked brand new and there were bright flags flying from the towers.

Amy rubbed one hand across her eyes. The castle was still there. She was riding along a road packed with people laughing and talking to each other. There were jugglers, people selling food, and at the side of the road a girl was herding a flock of geese. They hissed and squawked, stretching out their long white necks.

Amy blinked. Was this a different part of the fairground? Or was she dreaming? She stroked Brightheart's neck again. To her

delight, he looked round at her and gave an encouraging snort.

It wasn't just Brightheart who had changed, Amy realized. Her jeans and jumper had gone, and instead she was wearing a long dress made of green velvet. Her blonde hair, which had been in a ponytail before, hung loose around her shoulders. When she put up a hand to feel her head she discovered that she was wearing a delicate jewelled headdress, like the tiara she'd worn when she was a bridesmaid!

Amy felt very elegant in her dress, just like the princesses in her favourite book. She sat up a bit straighter.

"Oh, I'm so glad I decided to wear my new blue dress today!" said a voice behind her.

Amy looked over her shoulder. She was riding in a procession of other girls, all on the prettiest ponies she'd ever seen. They were all round her, and everywhere she looked there was another pony wrinkling its nose at her or giving a friendly shake of its mane. The girl in the blue dress was riding a dappled grey, and next to her was a girl on a lively chestnut mare.

"It is a lovely dress," agreed the girl on the chestnut. "This brown velvet of mine is looking a bit shabby. Watch out though, Eleanor. I saw Lady Isabella glaring at you just now. You know how cross she gets if anyone has a prettier dress than her." She nodded over her shoulder at a sturdy covered chair. There were thick red velvet curtains all the way around, hiding whoever was inside. The chair was carried by two guards, who were puffing along in studded leather armour. The armour looked heavy and Amy felt sorry for them because it was a very hot day.

Eleanor looked worried. "Oh dear, do you think she's jealous? I hope nothing's going to spoil the fun today! All the most famous knights in the kingdom will be at the jousting tournament. I hope Isabella doesn't get into one of her moods and spoil it."

Amy felt very excited. She had just learned about tournaments for her school history project, but she'd never dreamed she'd actually see one for real!

"Amy! Hey, Amy!"

Amy frowned. Who said that? Everyone she could see was admiring the procession or talking about the jousting. But Brightheart was tossing his head and jingling his bridle, almost as though he was trying to say something.

"Amy!"

There it was again, louder this time.

Amy looked at Brightheart. Brightheart glanced round at her quickly and twitched his ears, and then he went back to watching the road.

Amy gulped. Was her *pony* talking to her?

"Um, did you say something?" she whispered, leaning closer to Brightheart's ears and feeling a bit silly.

"Yes, I did! I've been trying to get your attention for ages!"

It was *definitely* the pony.

"You can *talk*!" Amy squeaked.

Brightheart tossed his head. "Of course I can! I'm not just any old carousel pony, you know. Anyway, all ponies can talk, it's just you humans that can't understand us! But you've got the magic carousel ticket with my name on it, so that's how you know what I'm saying."

19

"What, really and truly magic? Oh, this is so exciting!" Suddenly Amy felt worried. "What about Grandad? He must be wondering where I am."

"Don't worry, you'll be back before he even notices you're gone. That's part of the magic of the carousel." Brightheart pricked his ears back and his voice grew serious. "Amy, there's something I have to tell you. We've been brought here because we need to help someone. I don't know exactly who it is yet, but I know you're the right person because my name appeared on your ticket. The carousel magic found you for me! We're back in the Middle Ages, the time of knights and princesses and castles, and there's something very important that we have to do!"

3. Into the Forest

Amy couldn't believe what she was hearing. The Magic Pony Carousel had brought her here to help someone! With a talking horse! She would do her best, but she wasn't sure she knew enough about the Middle Ages to be much use. She hoped the Magic Pony Carousel hadn't made a mistake.

Brightheart snorted as if he knew what she was thinking. "Don't worry – the magic wouldn't have sent you if you weren't the right person. You'll see!"

Amy took a deep breath and nodded. But

who needed her help? She glanced sideways at the other girls in the procession, trying not to attract their attention. They all looked perfectly happy, chatting away about their favourite knights. But what about the person in the sedan chair? It was impossible to see her because she was behind the thick velvet curtains.

As Amy watched, a guard in front of the sedan tripped on a stone and the chair jolted.

The curtains flew back and a sharp-faced girl a few years older than Amy looked out. "What do you think you're doing, you fool? I'm not a sack of vegetables! Be more careful!"

"Yes, Lady Isabella," muttered the guard.

The girl on the chestnut pony gasped. "Lady Isabella! Are you all right? Did that stupid man jolt you?"

"Of course he did!" Isabella snapped. "Don't you have eyes in your head?"

"Never mind, my lady, we've nearly arrived," soothed Eleanor. "It's going to be a wonderful tournament! So many famous knights will be there! And it's Prince Henry's first joust. He'll be desperate to win with you watching, Lady Isabella."

Isabella pulled a face. "Prince Henry won't win. He's so clumsy. I know he'll want to dance with me at the banquet tonight and I just can't bear it." She sighed. "Last time we danced he trod on my toes so many times that my new slippers were ruined!"

Amy leaned forward and whispered to

Brightheart. "Do you think we are here to help Isabella?" She hoped not — Isabella was so bossy!

Brightheart shook his head, jingling his bridle. "No, I don't think she needs help with anything!" He gave a quick look around to see if anyone was watching, but all the girls were still fussing round Lady Isabella.

"Hold tight!" he called over his shoulder to Amy, and he set off at a brisk trot, dodging some children who were watching a man juggling apples.

"Where are we going?" Amy puffed, hanging on to Brightheart's mane. Trotting in a side saddle was very bouncy!

"Into the forest!" Brightheart replied. "We need to talk without arousing suspicion!"

The forest loomed beside the road that led from the castle to the jousting arena. It was *very* big. Amy felt a bit nervous as they left the road and entered the forest between two huge black trees. The noise from the road faded behind them and it felt much cooler in the shade. It was the sort of forest Amy had read about in stories, where you might find wolves and bears and witches and . . .

"Brightheart?" Amy's voice shook.

"Yes?"

"Are there any *dragons* in this forest?"

"Of course not!" Brightheart gave a

snort. Amy felt relieved – of course there was no such thing as dragons! But then he added, "Dragons live in caves in the mountains, not in forests like this."

Oh, so dragons *were* real . . . Amy gulped as she wondered just how big dragons were. She decided to keep an eye out for them, just in case. She might be in the time of knights and castles, but she didn't have anything useful like a sword. She spotted a flash of movement through the trees and her heart jumped into her mouth.

But it wasn't a dragon – it was another horse, a sturdy grey mare, not nearly as beautiful as Brightheart, but with friendly eyes. Amy breathed a sigh of relief.

Amy and Brightheart arrived at the edge of a clearing and stopped to watch. The mare's rider was wearing a suit of armour

and carrying a shield, but he seemed rather *small* to be a proper knight. The rider's helmet visor was tipped back so that Amy could see his face. He had fair hair and he looked about twelve years old – only three years older than Amy.

The boy held a long wooden lance under his arm. The point of the lance wobbled up and down. It looked as if it was far too heavy for him. He was trying to get the mare to gallop towards a target that was hanging from one of the trees. The target was a sack of straw, swinging on a rope.

The boy drummed his heels against the mare's side, but his pony didn't go any faster than a slow trot.

Suddenly a rabbit shot out from under a bush and the mare leaped sideways. The boy managed to cling on, but his helmet visor crashed down over his face. He pulled wildly on the reins and his horse galloped straight towards Amy and Brightheart!

"Look out!" Amy gasped.

Brightheart jumped aside just in time and the grey mare swerved the other way. This time the boy fell off, landing on the forest floor in a clatter of armour that sounded like someone dropping an armful of saucepans. His lance stabbed into the ground beside him and stayed there, quivering.

Amy scrambled down from Brightheart's back. The boy struggled to get up, weighed down by his armour, but Amy was too cross to help him. "Are you mad?" she shouted. "You could have been really hurt — and so could we!"

The boy managed to push his visor open. He lay on the ground, staring up at Amy as she told him off.

"You should learn to ride properly! And get a helmet that fits!"

She was just running out of breath when she realized that Brightheart was tugging at her sleeve with his teeth.

"Shh! You can't talk to him like that! That's a royal crest on his helmet. This must be Prince Henry, the king's son!"

4. A Right Royal Mess

Amy stopped. She turned to look at Brightheart. "Why didn't you tell me before I started shouting at him?"

Brightheart opened his eyes wide as if to say she hadn't given him much chance. Amy supposed he was right. She looked back at the boy, suddenly feeling worried. She had a nasty feeling that princes in the Middle Ages could order people to have their heads cut off!

Luckily, Prince Henry didn't look angry,

just puzzled. "Why are you talking to your horse?" he asked.

Amy glanced at Brightheart, but he was staring at the branches above his head as if he'd never dream of doing anything as silly as talking.

Amy thought for a moment. Brightheart had said that she could understand him because of the carousel magic – and that probably meant that everyone else just heard Brightheart whinnying, or saw him flicking his ears and wrinkling his muzzle. She turned back to Prince Henry and shrugged. "It's, um, a long story! I'm sorry that I was rude to you. I didn't know who you were, and . . ." She trailed off, not knowing what to say to a prince.

Brightheart nudged her from behind. "Curtsy!" he snorted.

31

"Oh!" Amy gathered up her long skirt and made a rather clumsy curtsy. It was quite difficult in the heavy velvet dress. As she struggled back up, she noticed that Prince Henry didn't look cross with her at all. Instead he was smiling.

"You weren't really rude," he said. "You're right — I'm no good at riding. But people don't usually tell me things like that."

Amy thought that sounded rather nice, but then she thought for a bit longer and decided that maybe it wasn't. "Not even your friends?" she said.

Henry looked glum. "I haven't got any friends. I mean, people want to be friends

32

with me, but I think most of them only like me because I'm a prince." So he *was* a prince.

Amy felt sorry for Henry. Being a prince didn't sound like much fun.

"And who are you?" asked Henry politely. Amy froze.

"My name is . . . Amy. Princess Amy from the Kingdom of Carousel. It's, er, far away . . ."

Both Brightheart and Henry looked at her quizzically.

"What were you trying to do with that sack?" Amy continued quickly, before Henry could ask her any more awkward questions.

"I'm practising jousting," Henry explained. "I've got to win the joust today you see. It's really important!"

"Why?" said Amy.

"Because it's a special joust. My father

has organized a competition with the sons of local knights and lords to give me a chance to take part. I really want him to be proud of me — but I'm just not very good." Henry sighed. "It's a lot to live up to being a prince, you know. *And* this girl I really like is presenting the prizes." He kicked miserably at a stone. "She thinks I'm stupid. She's beautiful, and good at dancing, and I'm so clumsy. Last time we danced, I trod on her feet about a hundred times."

Amy knew exactly who Henry was talking about. Lady Isabella! But why would someone as nice as Henry want to be friends with a girl like that?

"She just looks down her nose at me," Henry went on with a sigh. "Her nose is really pretty too," he added sadly.

Amy didn't know what to say. She hadn't liked Isabella at all. But she couldn't tell Henry that without hurting his feelings.

"Well, good luck in the tournament!" she said.

Amy led Brightheart over to a nearby tree stump. She needed something to stand on to get back into the saddle. "Come on, Brightheart, let's go and find the person who needs our help!" she whispered.

Brightheart jingled his bridle. "I think we should wait here," he said. "We need to make sure Prince Henry doesn't hurt himself!"

Henry mounted his grey mare and rode gloomily over to his lance. He tugged it out of the ground and tucked it under his arm, nearly dropping it twice. Then he began to trot towards the sack.

Amy held her breath. Would Henry hit the target this time?

Thwack!

Oh dear. If Henry had been *aiming* to hit that branch with the lance, it would have been a perfect strike . . .

Henry turned the grey mare round and tried again. This time the lance ended up in a blackberry bush. A couple of blackberries hit the ground with a juicy plop.

Amy had never done anything like jousting, but she was very good at sport and she could see that Henry was never going to hit the target at this rate. "You're not holding the lance tight enough!" she called. "Don't let the point fly up when you get close to the target!"

Henry gave her a long look, but he took his mare to the other side of the clearing for

a good run-up, gripped the lance and set off
again.

"That's it!" Amy called after him. "Lean
forward into it! Get your weight behind the
lance – oh no!"

Henry had leaned so far forward that
he'd toppled right out of the saddle. His
mare looked down at him with her ears

pricked back, as if she wondered what he was doing on the ground.

With a clank of armour, Henry stood up and stomped over to Amy and Brightheart. "I'd have hit it that time if you hadn't been shouting at me like that!"

Amy snorted. "You would not! You were miles out."

"Right then! If you think it's so easy, you do it!"

Amy was dying to have a go, but she wasn't sure if it would be OK with Brightheart.

"What do you think, Brightheart?" she whispered, trying not to move her mouth so Prince Henry wouldn't think she was talking to herself.

Brightheart tossed his head. "Of course we should have a go! After all, we can't be any more hopeless than poor old Prince Henry."

Amy stroked his neck. "Thanks, Brightheart!"

She turned back to Henry. "Pass me the lance, please," she said.

Henry handed it to her. It was heavier than Amy expected and she nearly dropped it. She remembered from her history lessons that in a real joust she would have to carry a shield as well!

She gathered up Brightheart's reins in her left hand. He started trotting towards the target and Amy lurched as the lance wobbled under her arm.

"Are you sure you want to do this?" Brightheart snorted.

Amy gripped the lance more tightly. "Yes! Come on!"

39

Brightheart broke into a canter and the sack came closer, closer . . .

There was a loud ripping noise as the lance went straight through the middle of the target.

"We did it!" Amy dropped the lance to give Brightheart a big hug.

Prince Henry looked astonished. "Well done!" He came over and scuffed at the ground with the toe of his metal shoe. "You should be riding in this tournament, not me. I'm just going to fall off in front of Lady Isabella."

Suddenly Amy had a brilliant idea. "Yes! I mean, why don't I?"

Henry looked up.

Amy beamed at him. "I can ride in the tournament instead of you!"

5. Princess Power

It was a fantastic plan! Amy loved doing sporty things, and she was never going to get another chance to be in a real live jousting tournament, nor get to be both a princess and a knight in one day!

Henry frowned. "Princesses can't joust," he said.

Amy pointed to the sack, which now had a big rip in it with lots of straw poking out. "They most certainly can! We've got a mixed football team at school, girls *and* boys, and I'm the top goal-scorer this season."

Henry looked confused and Amy realized that he wouldn't know what football was.

"That doesn't matter," she said quickly. "The thing is, I'm sure I could do it! With Brightheart's help," she added, leaning down to pat her pony. He snorted as if he knew exactly what she was saying – which, of course, he did.

Henry stopped frowning and looked thoughtful instead. "If you wore my

armour, no one would know you were a girl."

Amy gulped. Henry's armour didn't look very comfortable. "Can't I just wear the helmet?" she said.

"Of course not! You need the full suit of armour for jousting. Do you want to end up covered in bruises? Go and change out of that dress at once." Henry pointed towards a clump of bushes. For the first time, he sounded like a prince who was used to ordering people around.

Amy decided she liked him better when he wasn't being royal. "There's no need to be like that!" she said. "If you want me to help, you ought to be more polite."

Henry went bright red. "Sorry," he muttered. "It's really nice of you to do this for me."

Amy smiled at him. "Never mind –
go on, you get changed first." As Henry
went into the bushes to take off his armour,
Amy had a worrying thought. She slipped
off Brightheart's back and put her arm
around his velvety neck to talk to him
quietly.

"Is this OK, Brightheart? I got so excited
that I forgot the Magic Carousel had
brought me here to help someone. Shall I
tell Henry I've changed my mind?"

Brightheart shook his head. "Don't
worry. I think Prince Henry is the person
we are meant to be helping!"

There was a sound from the bushes like a
lot of tin cans falling over.

"Are you all right, Prince Henry?" Amy
called.

"Nearly ready!" Henry replied, sounding

flustered. "You can come and put the armour on now."

Leaving Brightheart standing beside Henry's grey mare, Amy pushed her way through the bushes.

Henry's armour was lying in a messy pile next to him, but he still had his long grey undershirt on.

"Are you sure I need to wear all this?" said Amy, looking down at the heap of armour.

"Oh yes," said Henry. "Otherwise you'd be in big trouble if someone caught you with the pole!"

Amy gulped.

"Go and take off your dress and put the leggings and this armoured doublet on," Henry said, a bit less bossily this time. He handed her a pair of scratchy-looking leggings and a weird padded jacket with bits of chain mail sewn on to it. "Then I'll help you into the armour. You'll never get it on by yourself. Even knights need their squires to help."

Amy nodded. She had learned about that at school. She never imagined she'd need a squire of her own!

She went behind a different bush to take her dress off – which was more difficult than she'd expected. It didn't have anything helpful like a zip, just lots of laces! She could hear Henry muttering impatiently on the other side of the bush as she wriggled out of the dress, and the underdress, and the funny sleeves that tied on. It took a long time to get out of the clothes.

Amy took a deep breath, then pulled on the leggings and heaved the chain-mail jacket over her head. It was very heavy and scratchy, but if it was going to stop her getting hurt, Amy didn't mind. She went to the other side of the bush so that Henry could help her with the rest of the armour.

"Right. We start at the feet and work up." Henry held up his long-toed metal shoes. "Sabatons first."

Putting on the armour was hard work. Amy could see that Henry was more used to having a servant help him than helping someone else. He got very muddled up with some bits, and for a while Amy had the breastplate upside down, which felt very uncomfortable indeed. But in the end she was dressed in a full suit of armour, just like a real knight!

"There you go!" said Henry, straightening her helmet and stepping back. "How does it feel?"

Amy tried to lift her arms. "Heavy. You really have to fight in all this?" Amy wasn't sure she could even walk, let alone carry a lance. It felt as if she had most of her mum's kitchen cupboard tied to her legs.

Henry grinned. "Yes. Come on, I'll give you a leg up. I've put Snowdrop's saddle with the royal crest on to Brightheart."

Amy slowly clanked over to Brightheart.

"You look just like Prince Henry!" he said, tossing his mane.

"Good," Amy puffed. She didn't have enough breath to say anything else. Moving around in armour was seriously hard work!

She stood on the tree stump, and Henry heaved her into the saddle with a lot of panting and complaining.

"Good luck!" Henry said as he passed the lance and shield up to Amy. "Remember not to take the helmet off! It's got my blue crest on, and the shield has my coat of arms, the blue lion, so everyone will think you're me. I'll set off for the arena now too. I should make it just in time if I run. I'll wave to you from the stands, Amy – you can do it! See you after the joust! And thanks!"

Amy spent a few moments working out how to hold the lance *and* the shield *and*

Brightheart's reins. Then she lifted the lance to salute Henry, and Brightheart set off at a trot back through the trees. They were going to fight in the tournament!

6. Amy in Action

"Oof! You weigh a ton," Brightheart muttered as they reached the road.

"I can't help that," said Amy. "Henry said I had to wear the armour."

She could see the jousting ring just up ahead of them. Bursts of cheering rang out from the crowd, and there was a sound of hoofs like thunder. They sounded like very big hoofs, belonging to a very big horse.

Suddenly there was a huge crashing noise. A knight had fallen off! Or rather

he'd been knocked off by his enemy's lance.
Amy started to feel a bit nervous.

"Brightheart?"

"Yes?" Was it her imagination or did he
sound nervous too?

"Have you done *lots* of jousting before?"

Brightheart hesitated. "Not exactly . . ."

"Um, have you done any at all?" Amy
asked hopefully.

"Well, I've watched quite a few
tournaments. It can't be that hard, can it?"

But by now they had reached the
jousting ring and there was no time left for
worrying.

A steward dressed in a bright red coat
rushed over to them. He had a long thin
trumpet tucked under his arm. "Where
have you been, Prince Henry? You're only
just in time!"

Amy opened her mouth to reply, then realized she would sound like a girl. She coughed and muttered "Sorry!" in a gruff voice.

Even though the visor made it hard to see clearly, there was something very familiar about the steward. He had the most twinkly eyes and Amy felt sure she'd seen him somewhere before.

Was it Mr Barker from the fairground, dressed in a red steward's coat? It *did* look like him, but what would he be doing here? The steward swept her a low bow. As he straightened up, he gave Amy a wink, as if he knew she wasn't Prince Henry at all.

Amy was just about to tell the steward she wasn't sure this was a good idea after all, when the huge wooden gates swung open. The jousting arena stretched ahead of them. There was a broad sweep of grass with a wooden barrier down the middle, surrounded by rickety-looking stands packed full of people.

When the crowd caught sight of Amy and Brightheart, they started cheering. "Look! It's Prince Henry!"

Amy gulped. It was too late to back out now!

The young knight who had lost the last round cantered out of the arena. His armour was dented and he shook his head miserably.

The scarlet-clad steward lifted his trumpet to his lips and blew a fanfare.

Brightheart jingled his bridle and snorted. The cheering was far too loud for Amy to talk to him. She patted him on the neck as gently as she could in her metal gloves, and they were off!

They cantered past the royal enclosure where the king was sitting. He looked like an older version of Henry, and very grand. He wore a blue doublet embroidered with little golden lions, and a dark blue velvet coat over the top. His grand wooden chair had lions carved into it as well, and they were on the banners flying above his head. Amy realized that the lions must be his family symbol – and she was carrying it too, on Henry's shield! She spotted Lady Isabella sitting in the same enclosure, looking bored and sulky.

"That horse isn't nearly as handsome as

my Beauty," Amy heard her say. "Henry's got no chance. He'll fall off as soon as he tries to gallop!" She laughed cruelly, and a thin-faced woman standing behind her frowned. Amy guessed she was Isabella's mother.

"Isabella, be quiet! The king might hear you!"

Lady Isabella just shrugged.

Amy gritted her teeth. It was time to show Isabella that "Prince Henry" wasn't as hopeless as she thought!

Brightheart stopped at the end of the arena and wheeled round, ready to charge towards their opponent.

Amy stared at the other knight in dismay. He looked older than Henry – and taller. He was wearing shiny black armour, with a helmet shaped like an eagle's head. His black horse was draped in grey livery and there was a long pointed spike sticking out from his bridle. Amy's tummy flipped over. This was going to be much more difficult than fighting Henry's sack of straw!

The steward blew into his trumpet again before lowering it. "On the black horse, we have Humphrey Greystone, squire to his father, the champion jouster Sir Humphrey Greystone!" he announced. "Undefeated after two bouts!"

The crowd cheered enthusiastically as Humphrey Greystone cantered over towards the royal box. He bowed in his saddle to Isabella and spoke loudly enough for everyone to hear:

"My lady! Will you give me the honour of fighting on your behalf?"

Isabella went bright red but looked really pleased. She leaned forward to pass Humphrey a white handkerchief, which he tied to the end of his lance.

"Good luck, Humphrey! Fight well for me!" said Isabella, and she giggled in a very irritating way.

"We *have* to win now!" Amy muttered to Brightheart. "But how can we? Just look at that Humphrey – he's enormous!"

"Exactly," Brightheart replied confidently. "He's big all right, but that means he'll be slow."

Amy felt a bit more hopeful. Brightheart sounded like her football coach, telling the team what tactics to use before a match.

"You can use his weight against him," Brightheart went on. "Honestly, I've seen lots of jousting, and bigger doesn't always mean better. When he leans over to strike at you, it'll take him ages to change direction if we nip back the other way. If we dodge around enough, we'll tire him out. You'll get points for a hit if your lance breaks on his shield, but what you really want to do is knock him off."

Amy nodded. Suddenly there was a blare of trumpets.

Brightheart sprang forward. As soon as they were galloping, Amy stopped feeling nervous. She kept her eyes fixed on Humphrey Greystone's shield. If she could hit it hard enough with her lance, in just the right spot, she might be able to push him out of the saddle.

The air filled with thundering hoofbeats as the massive black horse came closer. Humphrey's lance zoomed towards Amy's shield. Amy dodged, slipping her left foot out of the stirrup and leaning all the way over Brightheart's shoulder. Bright-heart leaned over with her, sensing what she needed him to do, and the lance scraped by. Amy managed a spilt-second glance at Humphrey Greystone's face through his visor as he galloped past. He looked angry.

"Phew! That was close! Well done, Amy!" Brightheart panted. He slowed down as she struggled upright again.

"We didn't hit him, but I think I know what to do next time. I need to stand up and lean much further forward," Amy puffed. "This is so exciting!"

The two riders lined up again, waiting for the trumpet blast. Now!

Up in the stirrups – forward with the lance – dodge – and strike! *Yes!*

There was a massive splintering noise and Amy's lance shattered against Humphrey Greystone's shield. Humphrey lurched backwards, but just managed to stay on. As they passed each other, Amy saw him turn to look back in disbelief, and she beamed behind her visor.

"Hooray for Prince Henry!" yelled the crowd.

The steward in the scarlet coat ran up with a spare lance. As he handed it to Amy, he said, "Well done! That was a great hit! Keep going."

Amy grinned back at him. She was almost sure he was Mr Barker. "Thank you! This is the best adventure *ever*!"

Brightheart snorted. "It's a pretty good adventure for me too!" he said.

Amy tightened her grip on the reins. "I'm really glad we're sharing it," she told him. "Come on, we've got one more chance to win!"

The trumpet sounded and the two horses charged towards each other again. Brightheart's hoofs hardly seemed to touch the ground. Amy felt him drawing all his strength into his shoulders, bracing himself for the impact. She shut her eyes. They were going too fast for her to see Humphrey's shield!

Thwack!

There was a deafening smack as lance met shield. Amy waited to be flung out of the saddle.

She opened her eyes. She was still on Brightheart, galloping across the grass.

Humphrey had fallen off!

The stewards rushed to pick him up, but he was already clambering to his feet, shaking his fist. The audience was cheering loudly for their prince.

A different steward in a green coat brought Amy a wooden beaker of water and she wondered what would happen next. Would she have to fight again?

Brightheart explained out of the corner of his mouth. "Now we'll have another couple of jousts, I think. It depends how many are fighting in this junior tournament. Oh look, here we go."

Their next opponent was trotting into the ring. He looked very confident, but amazingly he fell off before Amy even had a chance to hit him. It was partly his fault for showing off, because he threw himself out of the saddle trying to reach her with his lance.

The third boy wasn't such a pushover. He was almost as tall as Humphrey, but his horse was as fast and nimble as Brightheart. The first round was definitely his on points, as Amy had to drop her lance and shield and throw herself flat on Brightheart's neck just to dodge him!

The crowd gasped in dismay — they loved their plucky prince — but the gasp changed to a cheer as Amy stayed glued to her saddle. Luckily, the boy seemed to have a very short temper, and he flourished his lance wildly in the next round, determined to hit Amy properly this time. He was so off-balance that it took only an extra burst of speed from Brightheart and one well-aimed thump from Amy's lance — and he was gone!

The crowd roared so loudly that Amy's ears started to ring. She bent down and gave Brightheart's neck a hug. "You're doing brilliantly!"

Brightheart snorted. "Thanks! We make a pretty good team!"

The steward in scarlet walked into the middle of the arena and blew his trumpet. As the crowd fell silent, he announced, "Prince Henry – the champion!"

Amy and Brightheart had won the tournament!

7. A Prize Imposter

Amy couldn't believe it. They'd done it! Henry would be thrilled, and hopefully Isabella would be nicer to him from now on. Amy looked quickly round the stands to see if she could give Henry a wave, but there were so many people that she couldn't spot him.

The trumpets blared again as the green steward announced, "The winners will now receive their prizes from the king and his guest of honour, Lady Isabella!"

Oh no! Henry would have to collect the

prize. There was no way Amy could fool Henry's own father!

Amy bit her lip. Perhaps she could ask for a minute to tidy herself up first?

But it was no use. The friendly steward in the scarlet coat was nowhere to be seen. Instead, the steward wearing the green coat gave Amy an impatient look. "I'm sorry, Your Highness. Your royal father and the Lady Isabella are waiting for you."

Amy's shoulders slumped inside the armour. Thinking quickly, she checked that her visor was shut, so that her face was completely hidden, and rode towards the royal enclosure. She would just have to accept the prize and get out of there as fast as she could!

Brightheart didn't seem to be worried at all and kept tossing his head. He was obviously enjoying being the centre of attention.

Suddenly Amy spotted someone waving to her from the front of the crowd. It was Henry! He had made it and he'd seen them win! He'd borrowed a tunic from someone to wear over his underclothes — it was much too big and hung all the way down to his knees. He looked worried about Amy collecting the prize as well, but there was nothing they could do.

Isabella had a bored, sulky expression on her face. Amy guessed she was cross that Prince Henry had won — especially after she'd given her handkerchief to Humphrey Greystone. Amy dismounted and handed Brightheart's reins to a page who came running over, then walked up the steps to meet the king.

Isabella stood up, scowling, and took Amy's prize from a silver tray held by another page. It was a beautiful pair of gloves, not metal ones for jousting, but soft ones for wearing on special occasions. They were decorated with a wonderful pattern of birds and flowers in crimson silk and gold thread.

Amy was so busy admiring the gloves that she almost forgot she was supposed to be in a hurry. Brightheart whinnied to her from the bottom of the steps. "Quick, Amy! Before the king realizes you're not Prince Henry!"

Amy took the gloves, bowed to Isabella and started to hurry back down the steps.

"Not so fast, not so fast, son!" called the king.

Amy felt her heart sink. She walked reluctantly back to stand in front of the throne.

The king looked delighted. "My lords and ladies, I present to you my brave and brilliant son!" he declared to the people sitting around him. He leaned over and

gave Amy a massive clap on the back, which nearly knocked her over. She just managed to keep her feet, but her helmet flew off.

Amy gasped and scrambled to put her helmet back on. But it was too late. Her blonde hair had fallen down around her shoulders, and people in the crowd started to mutter.

"That's not the prince."

"Who is it?"

"Is that a *girl*?"

The king stared at her in astonishment. "Who are you? Where's Henry?"

Isabella stalked over to Amy, her eyes

flashing. "You little . . . ! What shameless game are you playing? Give me back those gloves and get out of here!"

Her voice had risen to an unladylike screech, but Amy didn't feel scared. Instead, she wanted to shout back. Isabella was so rude!

Suddenly someone dashed across the field and bounded up the steps.

"How dare you speak to her like that? Princess Amy is my friend!"

8. Henry Fights Back

It was Henry, still in his too-large tunic, but somehow looking more royal than Amy had ever seen him. He stood protectively in front of Amy, his eyes flashing, and Isabella's mouth fell open in shock.

The crowd whispered and nudged each other.

"Look, it's Prince Henry!"

"But who's that girl? Is she a princess?"

Henry heard them. "This is Amy," he said loudly. "She's the bravest girl I've ever met." He looked around at the crowd. "You saw her fight today. Didn't she deserve to win the tournament?"

A massive cheer rang out. "Yeeesss!"

Henry stood in front of the king. "Father, I asked Amy to take my place. You mustn't be angry with her. I wasn't good enough to fight. I'll try again next year, I promise!"

Amy looked anxiously at the king — would he be angry that they'd tried to trick everyone? Under his crown his handsome face was frowning — in confusion, in disbelief, in anger. Amy glanced at Henry, but he didn't look scared, he was standing tall and meeting his father's gaze.

At last the king shook his head and laughed. "Well, you found yourself a noble champion, my son."

From down on the field Brightheart

snorted approvingly, and Amy turned to grin at him.

"Amy has been a true friend to me, Father," Henry went on. He turned to Isabella. "I'm sorry for deceiving you, my lady. I wanted to show you that I was a great horseman, and one worthy of your friendship. But you have never been a friend to me like Amy has. In fact, you're – you're . . ." Henry's indignant speech trailed away.

Amy felt like adding "A spoilt brat!", but decided she'd better keep quiet.

Henry shrugged. "Well, you're no friend of mine, Lady Isabella. And don't worry, I won't ask you to dance this evening."

Lady Isabella gasped. Amy guessed what she was thinking. However much Isabella complained about Henry, he was still the prince and all her friends would be expecting him to dance with her. Isabella crept back to her seat, looking embarrassed. Her mother glared at her.

"Amy must be allowed to keep the prize, Father," Henry said firmly. "She won it fair and square!"

The king smiled. "Indeed she did. Well done, Amy."

Amy quickly bowed low.

The king went on: "Henry, I am very proud of you for defending Amy just now. It is a knight's true calling to defend those in trouble."

Henry blushed. "Yes, Father," he muttered. "I didn't really think about being a knight, though. I just didn't like Isabella shouting at Amy."

His father clapped him on the back. "Honest as well. We'll make a knight of you yet, my son."

Amy was so happy, she felt like turning cartwheels! She'd won the tournament and Henry had got a chance to prove to his father that he was as brave and honest as any knight.

Then she saw Isabella scowling at them and her heart sank. She and Brightheart had failed in their task after all! Isabella still didn't like Henry, and now Henry didn't like Isabella either!

A whinny from Brightheart interrupted her. Henry and his father were busy talking, so she went down the steps to see what was wrong. "What is it, Brightheart?"

The horse blew anxiously in her ear. "Come on, Amy! We've finished our task and the magic is going to take us back. I can feel it tugging at me already!"

Amy stared at him in surprise. "But, Brightheart, we've done it all wrong! Henry doesn't even like Isabella any more!"

Brightheart swished his tail. "Actually, you've done *exactly* what you were supposed to do. Henry needs to be a good judge of character if he's going to be king. You helped him to see that Isabella isn't quite as wonderful as he first thought. Quick, climb on, we haven't much time!"

Amy looked back at the royal enclosure. Henry certainly looked very happy. He gave Amy a cheerful wave when he saw her looking at him. Amy waved back.

The scarlet-clad steward appeared beside her. "Let me help you into the saddle," he said. "Then you can ride your lap of honour."

Amy started to protest that there wasn't time, that the Magic Carousel was pulling them back, but Brightheart whispered, "Do as he says! Quick!"

The steward gave her a leg-up and Amy scrambled into the saddle. Brightheart arched his neck and cantered proudly round

the arena. The crowd cheered, obviously delighted with their champion – even if she was a girl.

As she passed the royal box, Amy waved to Henry again. "Keep practising, Henry!" she called. "You can do anything if you try!" Amy had seen that for herself.

Brightheart started to gallop faster, until the arena and the crowd whirled into a dazzling blur. Brightheart's hoofs no longer seemed to be touching the ground. They were galloping through the air, galloping through a cloud of glittering sparkles.

And as the sparkles faded away, Amy realized that she was back at the fairground. Brightheart was a wooden horse once more, rising and falling as the carousel slowly turned. Grandad was standing on the grass, waving to her.

Her magical ride was over. The carousel stopped and Amy shook her head, dazed, as the last silvery sparkles vanished. She clambered down to give her pony one last hug.

"Thank you, Brightheart," she whispered. "Thank you for the most exciting adventure I could ever have. I'll never forget it."

Just for a moment, Brightheart's neck felt warm and real beneath her cheek. Then he was a wooden pony again, his beautiful dark coat nothing more than paint. But Amy was sure she could see an extra twinkle in his deep brown eyes. She felt sad that her adventure was over so soon, but just as she noticed that extra twinkle in Brightheart's eyes, she realized she was still clutching the beautifully decorated gloves she had won in the jousting tournament.

She would remember her ride on the Magic Carousel forever!

Log on to

Magic Pony Carousel

.com

for magical adventures, games and fun!

Jump on board the Magic Pony Carousel for a whole lot of fun! You can find out more about the Magic Ponies plus play fun pony games and download cool activities.

Log on now at

www.magicponycarousel.com

Collect three tokens and get this funky Magic Pony Carousel photo frame!

Magic Pony Carousel

www.magicponycarousel.com

There's a token at the back of each Magic Pony Carousel book – collect three tokens and you can get your very own, totally free Magic Pony Carousel photo frame!

Send your three tokens, along with your name, address and parent/guardian's signature (you must get your parent/guardian's signature to take part in this offer) to: Magic Pony Carousel Photo Frame Offer, Marketing Dept, Macmillan Children's Books, 20 New Wharf Road, London N1 9RR

erms and conditions apply: Open to UK and Eire residents only. Purchase
f three MAGIC PONY CAROUSEL books is necessary. Offer not open to
ose over the age of twelve. Please ask permission of your parent/guardian
enter this offer. One photo frame per entry and per household. Actual
hoto frame may differ from one shown. Size of frame is 100 x 100mm. No
roup entries allowed. Photocopied tokens will not be accepted. Photo
ames are distributed on a first come, first served basis, while stocks last.
o part of the offer is exchangeable for cash or any other offer. The closing
ate for this offer is 31/12/06. Please allow 28 days for delivery. We will use
ur data only for the purpose of fulfilling this offer. We will not pass
formation on to any third parties. All data will be destroyed after the
romotion. For full terms and conditions, write to: Magic Pony Carousel
hoto Frame Offer, Marketing Department, Macmillan Children's Books,
0 New Wharf Road, London N1 9RR

Magic Pony Carousel Photo Frame Offer

1 Token

Collect 3 tokens and get your free photo frame!
Valid until 31/12/06

Star

Poppy Shire

The carousel music grew louder and the horses swooped through the air as they gathered speed. The breeze blew on Laura's cheeks and the fairground lights seemed to glitter and twinkle around her. To her surprise the breeze felt warm, like on a summer's day, and the air began to glow and shimmer like summery mist. She looked up and gasped. It was no longer a cool autumn evening – instead the sky was a beautiful bright blue, with the sun blazing down. And she wasn't holding on to the golden pole any more. She had real leather reins in one hand and a rope lasso in the other!

Books coming in 2006

The prices shown below are correct at the time of going to press. However, Macmillan Publishers reserves the right to show new retail prices on covers which may differ from those previously advertised.

March

| Magic Pony Carousel: Sparkle | 0 330 44041 1 | £3.99 |
| Magic Pony Carousel: Brightheart | 0 330 44042 X | £3.99 |

June

| Magic Pony Carousel: Star | 0 330 44043 8 | £3.99 |
| Magic Pony Carousel: Jewel | 0 330 44044 6 | £3.99 |

October

| Magic Pony Carousel: Crystal | 0 330 44597 9 | £3.99 |
| Magic Pony Carousel: Flame | 0 330 44598 7 | £3.99 |

All Pan Macmillan titles can be ordered from our website, www.panmacmillan.com, or from your local bookshop and are also available by post from:

Bookpost, PO Box 29, Douglas, Isle of Man IM99 1BQ
Credit cards accepted. For details:
Telephone: 01624 677237
Fax: 01624 670923
Email: bookshop@enterprise.net
www.bookpost.co.uk

Free postage and packing in the United Kingdom